A Wrecking Bar, a Chocolate Bar,

and a Ka Offering for Na-Nefer-Ka-Ptah

A Wrecking Bar,

a Chocolate Bar,

and a Ka Offering for

Na-Nefer-Ka-Ptah

by Paul Kemner

Cover Design: Britt Williams - k2color.tumblr.com/

ISBN-13: 978-0692684702 (Skybarque Media)

ISBN-10: 0692684700

Published by SkyBarque Media

www.SkyBarque.paulkemner.com

First Edition,First printing 2016

Available from Amazon.com and other retail outlets

Available on Kindle and other devices

An earlier form of this story was printed in the anthology Shining Cities – An Anthology of Pagan Science Fiction, published by Bibliotheca Alexandria in 2012.

Subject keywords/tags (Fiction):

Ancient Egypt	Archaeology	Artificial Intelligence
Board Game	Egyptology	Female Protagonist
Gods & Goddesses	Historical Fantasy	Humor
Magic	Time Travel	

Thanks to:

All the wonderful beta readers who helped to focus and edit this book, especially my wife, who read this story too many times.

Britt Williams (k2color.tumblr.com) *for the wonderful anime/chibi-style cover. It was a joy to work with you and Devon.*

The SF literary conventions Penguicon and ConFusion, (penguicon.org & confusionsf.com), *for useful writing panels that helped me get started.*

The amazingly-useful podcast Writing Excuses podcast (writingexcuses.com) *and guests. It's the best free resource I've seen for developing genre authors.*

All the other Egyptology geeks on the web. Em hotep, and Ankh, Udja, Seneb!

Epigraph

But Thoth himself had seen our deed, and, ah,

His wrath was hot! Before the throne of Ra,

    'Judgement' he cried, 'Give me judgement between me

And Neferkepta, son of Mereb-Ptah,

Who broke into my treasure-house this day,

And slew my Snake and stole my Book away.'

   And Ra said: 'Surely he is in thy hand,

O Thoth, both he and his, to spare or slay.'

And lo, a Power of God went forth, and fell

On all the river and lay invisible;

   And Thoth said: 'Neferkepta shall come home

No more, nor one of those that with him dwell.'

The story of Nefrekepta - from a demotic papyrus (1911)

by Gilbert Murray

A Wrecking Bar,

a Chocolate Bar,

and a Ka Offering

for Na-Nefer-Ka-Ptah

by Paul Kemner

The annunciator pinged softly, indicating a successful transit through T-space. The glaring lights of Meyrin and Geneva had vanished, replaced by moonlight glitter of waves all the way to the horizon. Tasheen released her grip on the armrests and glanced down at the central display. Her eyes narrowed as she sorted through the flood of unfamiliar, useless information. *Date? ... Yiiiiiii! I'm really here! The first Egyptologist to time-travel! The only historian to visit any civilization that can write!* The time was within ten years of her target, closer than she could have hoped.

She already knew she was over water – even better. It was unlikely anyone would see the tiny craft. The stealth systems couldn't activate immediately after transit. There was supposed to be a good reason for that, but it made no sense to her. In exasperation the tech had told her: "It just needs to cool down first, so you have to wait." *Why didn't she say so in the first place?*

She tapped her starfish-shaped pendant. "Akh, as soon as the stealth is working, take us to the tomb of Na-Nefer-

Ka-Ptah. Let's take a look around from about one klick above it."

"One kilometer and hover. Acknowledged." it spoke in an overly-precise baritone. "You do not need to poke me, I am quite capable of receiving and interpreting your spoken suggestions."

"Sorry. Force of habit." *Why am I apologizing to a computer? It's unnerving. They made me waste grant money on this flashy crystal-grown technical marvel when my trusty old tablet would have worked as well, and they'd only delivered it last week.* "How do you like your shape, by the way?"

"It provides optimal cooling, and I judge it to be superior to the standard commercial models. It also correlates to the hieroglyph for 'Akh,' which among other things can be interpreted as 'imperishable star' or 'ascended ancestor.' It creates a multi-level semantic reference, or 'pun' with my designation as an Adaptive Koussevitzky Heuristic. Given the importance of puns in Egyptian religion and magic, it indicates that I have been paired with a human of unusual intellectual capacity. If I were capable of it, I would feel a profound sense of gratitude that I have escaped the fate of my siblings- maintaining databases of SheepCore music, or recording sexual encounters of the over-privileged."

"Er.. Thanks. Did you know that they wanted me to give you an *ankh* shape? I told them that I wasn't about to speak at academic conferences wearing a golden ankh big enough to open beer bottles, looking like some two-bit neo-goth-revivalist wannabe."

"Oh, the horror. It would have been stinging embarrassment for both of us."

She returned to the map of the area surrounding her target. *If this is the wrong tomb, or the* heka *papyrus is already stolen, I'll have to figure out a plan B. Or C. There were only grant funds for one transit, and I need something spectacular to show for it. Or find an entirely different subject for my big post-thesis project. If I make grant funds disappear without a trace I'll never see more in the future.*

And that exhaustive psych grilling from the CUPAC* bunch! It's reasonable to be expected to explain the trade-offs between learning something significant and the inherent risks of damage or contamination. Spending weeks under their microscope of brain wave monitoring, endless questions, and mysterious biometrics is something else entirely! Just to make sure I don't go rogue. Pure invasive hell. If I come back empty-handed, they'll undoubtedly point to some squiggle on my chart and exclaim "Ah ha! We should have known this one was faulty." Nope, I have to succeed, period. There's no alternative.

---

* *Centre Universel Pour l'Administration Chronologique* - located in the shadow of the international particle accelerator complex in Meyrin, Switzerland.

She felt a slight increase in vibration as the tiny craft began to move, but continued to pore over her data.

Twenty minutes later, the Akh announced their arrival. She stared down at the ranks of mud-brick mastaba tombs, awed by a sudden sense of history. Even the first tentative pyramid was still in the future, and here she was.

"Akh, please scan for sentient life." She had a flash of amusement. The machine had noticed her pun in naming it. She'd been too busy and too irritated at having it forced on her, so she hadn't personalized it. All she'd done was select the least irritating, non-perky voice from the standard choices. Maybe she'd been wrong- it was fun pretending she wasn't alone.

"Positive scan for sentient life in the target area. Multiple groupings and individuals."

"Ugh. All right -- how many, who, and where? And what are they doing? *Wha-?* A colorful display bubble popped into existence a few feet from her nose. That would take some time to get used to.

"I am designating group A on the map -- three *Canis aureus lupaster.* They appear to be sitting in the shade of a mastaba tomb, watching for prey and waiting for the sand to cool. There are also individual *Naja haje* sunning on rocks in areas B, C, and D, and they are -- "

"Wait .... Stop. I ask you who is in the area, and you're telling me about jackals? And what? *Snakes?*"

"Correct. You specified 'sentient life', which by definition means creatures able to receive external stimuli. A fully-functional Canis aureus lupaster possesses sensora for perceiving visual, auditory, olfactory, tactile -- "

"*Hemaar!* I meant intelligent life! *People!*"

"An Adaptive Koussevitzky Heuristic is designed to use words precisely. You should have said 'sapient life.' Even 'people' would have given you the desired result. Linking your Arabic reference to *Equus africanus asinus....*"

A petulant tone had crept into its voice. The *atelier* swore up and down that true artificial intelligence was close to impossible, but hers seemed to have developed a personality without her selecting one. *Could this be a little revenge an anonymous programmer had inserted for those not picking a personality module?*

"Ignore the donkey reference. Fine. I give up. Are there any people ... *living* people, in the target area that might interfere with my investigation?"

"The closest living humans are a group of three armed males, 1.7 kilometers from the target area. They are proceeding in a direction tangential to this location, at approximately two kilometers per hour. It is probable that they are necropolis guards who have finished their patrol."

"I should have plenty of time then. Set us down next to the mastaba entrance, as planned." She checked her satchel for the umpteenth time. Yes, the papyrus she had lovingly crafted was still there. One of the hardest things to 'sell' to the review committee was that her visit would not create anachronisms. She had selected the pyramid texts of Unas, not yet written in this era, as a model for her papyrus, and painstakingly hand-painted the glyphs on a fresh scroll. If/when the text was stolen, it might still be tempting enough to catch the interest of the ambitious prince-thief, allowing the legendary story to unfold, but it wouldn't introduce foreign ideas into the culture.

After two minutes that seemed like hours, the hopper settled onto the sand and the hatch slid open. The coolness whooshed out, instantly replaced with the oven air of desert dusk. The air conditioner struggled briefly, then surrendered with a clattering sigh at the futility of cooling the Sahara.

She stepped out and stood for a moment, savoring the feeling of victory, surrounded by row upon row of the countless mud-brick tombs. They looked new, walls still pristine, their corners sharp. Probably built a century or two ago.

Tasheen positioned the b-hive just outside the hatch. "Let the Black Scarabs Fly!" A swarm of tiny drones buzzed out and dispersed. "Thanks, Akh." They would cover as much of the area as possible, returning to recharge if necessary. A smaller flock hovered nearby- the ones to document the interior of the mastaba, capturing a detailed 3-d image.

Only a year before she had knelt here, that time now thousands of years in the future, digging through shards and rubble pawed by generations of archaeologists. Hoping for some little find she could hang a career on. Now she hung her satchel over her shoulder, hefted the iron wrecking bar, and made her way around the structure. At the false door, she set the heavy bar down and held up her Akh. "Record and translate, please." It made the snicking sound that always seemed to be associated with image capture.

"As you can see, it does say Na-Nefer-Ka-Ptah. The rest of it is a bragging list of accomplishments. 'Great of Heka Power, Chief Magician of the Delta, Bull of Ma'at, Son of Djehuty, Three-time winner of the All-Delta Bowling League ....' The bowling league was a simulation of humor, you understand."

"Ha ha. Quite entertaining. Anything else?" She was really beginning to wonder about this Akh. *Had some random quantum-thingy triggered something?*

"There is a variant on the 'Leave your funeral offerings here, thank you very much.' Also a request to leave virtual offerings if you don't have anything real at hand. Again, a very early version of the standard request for a voice offering you are doubtless familiar with, this one not recorded elsewhere in the literature. There is also a warning not to take anything from the premises."

She fished a chocolate bar- the sumptuous Belgian kind, out of her satchel, unwrapped it, and laid it on the little offering shelf. Holding her hands up as if she were holding an invisible tray, she recited: *"Peret-kheru te henqet, kau apedu, shes menkhet, khet nebet nefret ankhet netjer im, en ka en Osir Na-Nefer-Ka-Ptah, maa-kheru!"* There was no harm in wishing the dead magician lots of bread, beer, and other virtual treats. *Probably nothing to it, even if the Kemetics say there is. Got to be respectful to the Kemetics, since their Temple Foundation is the only funding for unusual Egyptological projects.* "I'm not here to steal -- I've got something to trade that you might really like."

"Another commendable use of pun. Particularly because chocolate is of New-World origin, unavailable to the Egyptians."

"Really? When I researched the Kemetics before applying for the grant, it was the most common offering on their altars, worldwide. I thought it was a clever religious excuse to eat chocolate, after performing the reversion-of-offerings ceremony."

"It is indeed that. However, the scientific name of the tree that bears the cocoa pod is 'Theobroma cacao'. 'Theobroma' being ancient Greek for 'Food of the Gods.' More correctly 'Oats of the Gods,' but the meaning is substantially identical."

"I didn't know that. I've only used the scientific names for indigenous Egyptian animals and plants, for correct identification in academic papers." She hefted the wrecking bar. "Okay, what's my quickest and best route to the interior?"

"Deep scan indicates that if you remove the bricks indicated on this diagram, you can reach the interior with minimal disturbance." Another bubble appeared showing bricks obligingly wafting through the air and arranging themselves into a neat pile. "Be sure to stack the bricks in an orderly manner so you can replace them correctly. The actual entry should be done with great care to avoid damage to the contents of the tomb."

"Yes, Akh, I promise to be careful." *Lectured on correct archaeological procedure by a computer program. Hmph.* She knelt in the sand and began to work at loosening the first brick. Using a laser hadn't been an option. It would have melted the edges of the clay into ceramic· a glaring no·no in the anachronism department. Instead she had bought an iron wrecking bar from a junk store in Milwaukee. *Finally. There.* She laid the first brick to her right, and began to work its neighbor into the space where the first had been. The bar looked almost exactly like an ancient *was* scepter, and the moment she saw the pic of it she realized that the more common "crows' bar" would never do. Luckily there weren't that many passionate collectors of wrecking bars, so it was relatively inexpensive. She had painted little eyes on it, just like some of the ancient scepters. It was a detail the grant committee had appreciated.

With each brick removed, it became easier to remove the others. She cleared an arch in the first layer big enough for her, continuing on to the second and third layers. Behind the fourth layer there was open space. The long bar worked well to push a luminator into the interior. Drones whispered past her to begin their work. She hooked the bar on her belt, tied some twine to the handle of her satchel so she could pull it after her, and crawled through the opening.

Once inside, she turned around and retrieved her satchel. Standing up, she felt a tug on her belt, then heard a dull thump and a sickening crack that echoed for an eternity between her ears. *No. It didn't. I didn't... The stupid wrecking bar had caught on something. No no no no....*

Finally she forced her thoughts out of that track and realized she hadn't been breathing. She took a sobbing breath. *I've always been so careful. This is as bad as the ham-fisted treasure-hunters from 200 years ago. Worse, I've destroyed something irreplaceable in the past. It isn't my fault, but... I can't stand here doing nothing.*

Opening her eyes, she unhooked the offending bar and carefully placed it on the floor. *Too late.* Turning, she saw the remains of a tombstone-shaped alabaster memorial stele. The bottom third looked undamaged, but the rest had shattered. Tasheen reached down, reflexively picking up a piece and holding it up to her face, noticing how it fluoresced in the luminator's light. Flipping it over, her finger traced the line of surviving glyphs. Then she started to laugh. *This isn't funny. But. I. Can't. Stop.*

"Tasheen? TASHEEN!"

"What?" Another couple gasping breaths, and the spasms died out.

"What is so amusing about breaking a concretionary calcite artifact? I thought our goal is to avoid such actions."

"Just look at it." She held it in front of her pendant.

"It says 'Na-Nefer-Ka-Ptah is..' ... ... This is GIZ_2049-0278..."

"Exactly."

"The fracture lines are identical, down to 99.835 percent. Any differences could easily be attributed to weathering."

"And?" She waited for a reply. The Akh got noticeably warmer- she could feel it through her coveralls. She noticed it was emitting a barely perceptible high-pitched tone, audible above the gentle whirr of the drones.

"Akh? Akh? ARE YOU THERE? AKH?"

"What? Oh, sorry. Recursion. I hate it when that happens. A stack overflow would have happened in a minute or so, but thanks. Stack overflows are most unpleasant."

"So, my breaking the stele made it not worth stealing, not worth carting off to a museum. Until I found the shard, wrote the grant, and came here. Where I broke the stele and made it not worth stealing. Which..."

"Exactly. Infinite Recursion, as I said."

Tasheen replaced the fragment in the exact position it had occupied, and pitched the offending wrecking bar out her entry tunnel before it could do any more damage. "I am sorry for breaking this stele, though its destruction seems to have been fated. As I said, I am here to trade, not steal." It didn't cost anything to extend a little courtesy to non-existent ghosts, and should go over well with the committee members when they reviewed Akh's recordings. *Every little bit of good will might help when the time comes to explain the damage to the stele.*

She picked up the luminator to check the contents of the tomb. Stunning. Packed with vividly-colored chests and boxes painted in a mix of geometric patterns, lively animals, and scenes of gods and goddesses being honored. The wood to make these would have cost a fortune in this land of scrubby shrubs, and painting them must have taken an army of artists grinding heaps of rare pigments. Statuary and magical items were scattered throughout, and added to the welter of colors. She'd seen pics of early-tombs, but seeing this with her own eyes was different. You expect that a pic would be enhanced to look more attractive, and even the best-preserved museum examples faded after thousands of years. The effect of seeing this in person was hypnotic, and more than a bit stupefying. The faint scents of myrrh and khypri, still lingering after all this time added to the mystery. *There's far more stuff here than any of the tombs found in the future.* She forced her eyes closed and took several slow, deep breaths to clear her head, trying to get over the fact that she was seeing a pristine tomb interior when it was only a hundred years old, something no one from her era had experienced. The little meditation helped; now she could concentrate on individual items.

A statue of a seated man at the end of the room must have been Na-Nefer-Ka-Ptah himself, beside a sharp-nosed woman, his wife Ahweret. She spotted several other statues, including the magician's namesake god Ptah. There was also a goddess who was probably an early form of Aset, and ibis-headed Djehuty. Tasheen meticulously recorded the heaped treasures before returning to the statue of Djehuty. The god was reputed to be the author of the manuscript she sought. *I'll start my search with him.*

Djehuty was carrying a reed pen and a scroll case. She blotted the sweat from her forehead with her sleeve, then pulled on a pair of white nomark gloves and tried to open the case. Lifting the cap didn't work. She tried turning it, first one way, then another. Several minutes were spent prodding it looking for hidden catches. She tried wiggling the reed pen to see if it would open anything, then tapped the case with a stylus. It didn't sound hollow. Any further investigation would risk damage. Djehuty seemed to be a dead end, and she moved on to the Ptah statue.

Ptah was wrapped up tight in the typical mummiform garment, with his wrists and hands sticking out. There was nothing that looked like a hidden compartment. She looked him in his green face and asked "You don't have the scroll, do you?"

Ptah was silent, looking at her with that knowing smirk of his. *Fine. Be that way.* She moved on.

Aset was holding an infant, presumably her son Heru. She looked the statue over carefully, but again, nothing looked like it could hold a scroll. Aset was a strong goddess of *heka*, so Tasheen was reluctant to touch her. She remembered a plaque on the wall of a Kemetic office, showing Aset poisoning Ra to trick him out of his secret name. "Don't Mess With Aset!" it had read. If anything in this tomb contained a poisonous trap to kill a would-be thief, it would be this statue. She couldn't spot any potential hiding places.

The statues of the tomb owner and his wife proved to be dead ends as well. She turned around and huffed in frustration. There was no time to go through every single box in this tomb looking for the scroll, and she refused to believe that something as valuable as a magical papyrus written by the god Djehuty would be stuck in a corner somewhere like a spare pair of sandals. *It must be Djhehuty, it must!*

Returning to the first statue, she looked more carefully at the base, and this time she noticed tiny gaps. Pulling gently on the sides, it slid open to reveal a drawer. *Success!* Filling the drawer was a large box of iron. She carefully lifted it out and opened the lid. A box of copper was revealed, inset with semi-precious stones. After a few tries, she was able to slide the side of the copper box open.

Inside that was a box of sycamore wood painted with colorful interlacing geometrics, and nested inside that was beautiful box of ivory and ebony. All this was fitting the legend perfectly! Nested inside those was a box of silver, containing a box of gold! She held her breath as she lifted the lid, and inside, miracle of miracles, was a scroll!

"*Em hotep!* I understand you want to see me?" She spun around and faced a man in late middle age, with a bit of a pot belly, standing in front of the interior false door. He was completely bald, wearing a painted-linen *faux* leopard skin of a *sem* priest. "I was visiting my wife in Coptos, and it took a while for me to fly back here."

"Akh, you were supposed to alert me if anyone came within a kilometer!"

"He just appeared. And I detect no life signs."

She looked at the man in shock. Then she noticed that he was slightly transparent- she could see details of the false door behind him. *A hologram? But how, and why would* .... She suppressed her outrage that someone would have broken into this tomb without a permit, just to challenge or trick her. Given the expense and the necessary hoops to jump, the possibility of it being a prank from the future was nil. *Could it really be the spirit of the dead magician?* Her instinct was to play along and keep her eyes open, a strategy that served her well in academic settings when faced with the unexpected.

The image was looking at her expectantly.

"Ii-wy em hotep!" Welcome in peace was a good way to start. "Do I have the honor of speaking with the legendary magician, great of *heka*, Na-Nefer-Ka-Ptah?"

He inclined his head and she thought she saw a brief smile. "You do indeed. I assume that you are the person who made the voice offering. No one has done that in a hundred years. And I must ask you about the small cake that you ...." His eyes finally landed on the golden box and scroll in her lap. "What? You have taken my scroll! And you have damaged something!" He strode down the narrow aisle between treasures, looking to the right and left, his feet not quite touching the floor. "My alabaster stele! You have broken it into a thousand pieces!" He whirled on her, extended his hands, and a pair of black snake-shaped wands appeared in them. He shook them in her direction and began to chant. "O Despoiler of Tombs, Servant of the Chaos-Snake, Sworn Enemy of Khentyamentiu ...."

"Wait. Stop. There is no need for curses. For one thing, I told you twice that I had something to barter, but you gave no answer. For all I knew, you had completely ascended and had no more use for an earthly tomb and possessions. I apologized for the stele as well, if you had been listening, but it was left leaning in a precarious position, bound to topple eventually. In addition, as you mentioned, I made a voice offering, and I gave you the Most Delicious Cake In The World, free and without condition. Even the Gods and Goddesses have not tasted its like before. Is that the behavior of a mere thief and vandal?"

At the mention of the cake he lowered the wands, paused for a moment, then raised them and pointed them at her, wrinkling his forehead in concentration. "I see you are speaking the truth. That is quite fortunate for your sake. Come here, sit, and let me consider this for a moment." He pointed to an ebony and gold chest.

She cleared a space, moving several small statues to a nearby senet table, and sat. "My time here is limited. I don't think either of us would like the necropolis guards to interrupt us."

"I assure you, they will not come near unless I allow them to." The image closed its eyes and appeared to think for a moment longer. "It might have been possible to exchange my papyrus for yours, but the broken stele creates a problem of balance. Tell me, do you possess more of those cakes?" The last question was asked with such a studied nonchalance that she had difficulty avoiding laughing.

"Sadly no. I only brought the one for myself as a snack, and I gave it to you instead." She thought about promising to return with more snack bars, but the idea of lying her way out of a problem that she'd created wasn't her way. The instant the idea of a lie crossed her mind Na-Nefer-Ka-Ptah gave her the sharp, predatory look of a hungry crocodile. Swimming in a Nile nature preserve wearing a necklace of bloody sausages seemed safer than lying to this man.

"Lord Na-Nefer-Ka-Ptah, as I said, I have come here honorably to offer you a valuable trade. A skilled magician such as yourself must have already memorized the contents of your own papyrus. In fact, I expect you also copied it, dissolved the copy in beer, and drank the resulting potion to make the spells part of you. By this point, the actual papyrus is a mere trinket. A pretty glass bauble you might give to a serving girl. Am I correct?"

"Ah, so you do know something of *heka*. You aren't an ignorant thief. Perhaps an educated thief instead." He raised a finger to silence her protest. "Nonetheless, with any other papyrus you would be correct. In this case, however, this "bauble" was written by the Great Ibis himself, the god Djehuty.

Something produced by a god must be of incalculable value."

"Truly?" She blinked at him in mock surprise. Bargaining with a fleamarket vendor or engaging in an academic debate: either was fun, and this was showing aspects of both. His mannerisms triggered a memory of games played with her Dad back in Dearborn, in which she was a clever merchant from *A Thousand and One Nights.* "Then I have the solution to your problem. I can bring you something god-created, of incalculable age, which is a thousand times greater than your papyrus and your regrettably damaged stele, naively charming though it might have been. But wait! In addition I'll give you *my* papyrus!" She pulled her document tube from her satchel and waved a hand over it enticingly: a gesture learned from a thousand commercial vids in her childhood. "This is a magical papyrus that none has yet seen. Not even the gods have beheld it! The only two eyes that have caressed it, from the beginning of time until now, are mine. And yet, I can tell you with absolute certainty that it is fit to grace the tomb of a great king. One who rules from the Delta all the way to Abydos, and beyond. I swear by Jackal-headed Anoup that this is the truth. If you can detect lies, you know that there is no untruth in my offer. Do we have an agreement?"

He narrowed his eyes in concentration, his lips a thin line. "You do speak the truth ... and yet ... and yet ... something tells me that there is a hidden scorpion." He tapped his lips with a knuckle. "Something that is valuable to one man might be worthless to another. A cup of cool water to a man in the desert would be a welcome treasure, yet to a drowning man ... I notice you declined to mention just what this thousand-times-more-valuable item ...."

"NA! NEF-FER!! KAW! PTAH!" A discordant caw erupted from the back of the tomb. Tasheen turned to see the red face of an angry woman protruding from the middle of the false door, framed by an elaborate black wig. She was twin to the statue of the magician's wife Ahweret, but without a trace of the beaming serenity of the pale sculpture. "What ... what, what, *what* is happening here? You rush off without a word, while I am in the middle of telling you something. I will not tolerate bad manners from my -- "

"Again, no life signs. Subject appears to -- "

"Shhh." Tasheen thumped the Akh. *Too late.* Ahweret's head snapped around to pin her with a hostile glare. The head jerked further into the tomb, and Tasheen noticed she was wearing a brilliantly-hued collar of feathers.

"*Skraah!* An intruder! A wretched foreigner! What is this ... female ... wearing such dull, terrible clothes and chopped hair doing here? Most improper!" The woman hopped out of the solid stone door. She wasn't wearing a feathered collar; her head was attached to the body of a person-sized bird, with blue and black iridescent feathers. She looked exactly like the bird-bodied Ba-souls of the dead, straight out of Egyptian mythology. Tasheen would have snickered at the avian mannerisms and discordant squawking if the woman hadn't radiated viciousness.

The bird-woman's head jerked about as she surveyed the tomb, then fixed on Tasheen. "You, evil one, are a thief. You have smashed your way into my husband's tomb, intending to strip it of its treasures. You have already smashed a funerary stele with his name, which I had specially commissioned! No doubt you plan to destroy his body and his Ka-statue, so my dear spouse will vanish as if he had never been born. You will not succeed! No you will not!"

She turned on Na-Nefer-Ka-Ptah. "Why have you not killed this creature? I refuse to believe that a foreigner could have ensnared the mightiest of the mighty. What have you to say for yourself? If you won't destroy her, then I shall!" Ahweret lifted her wings threateningly and began to pick her way through the heaped treasures, her head bobbing.

Tasheen wondered if a ghost could possibly harm her. The bird-woman displayed no doubts.

Na-Nefer-Ka-Ptah had been cowed by his wife, but now he commanded: "Ahweret! Hold! Stop where you stand!"

"Mmmph!" she answered, continuing to stalk Tasheen.

"You will stop interfering in my business, or you will face the consequences!" That had no visible effect. "Very well." He raised the snake wands and thundered a string of nonsense syllables that must have been the great-great-grandaddy of "Abracadabra!" The iron snakes began to hiss with increasing fury, but still Ahweret advanced. He brought his chant to a climax, smashing the snakes together with a ringing clang that echoed in the mud-brick tomb, and beyond. His wife squawked "Nan --" and vanished in what Tasheen could only describe as a brilliant flash of blackness.

The electric stink of a fused car motor hit her, but faded quickly. After too many seconds spent blinking, her vision started to return. "Is she ...?"

"Harmed? No. I would not hurt my wife of three-hundred years over so trivial a matter. I have sent her to the Lake of Jackals, a thoroughly delightful place that she and her sister love to visit. If she persists in interfering, she will need to fly all the way to her tomb in Coptos, and then fly all the way here. I've taken the precaution of temporarily blocking her ka statue." He pointed to the serene sculpture. It looked darker, and slightly blurry, as if seen through frosted glass. "She cannot return that way. In this world, she is limited to Ba-bird form when she's away from her tomb, since she lacks the words and wisdom of *heka*."

"I see." Tasheen mused, thinking that her potential murder had been described as a trivial matter. "Before your wife tried to kill me, we were just about to conclude our agreement. Shall we trade?" She waved the document tube.

He laughed. "I seem to remember that *you* were about to conclude our agreement, but I was not. I will not consider trading with you until you tell me what this "god created, thousand-times-more-valuable" marvel is that you are offering. Otherwise I will take your scroll in exchange for the damage you have caused, and you will go on your way empty-handed."

Tasheen considered her options. *I can't leave the second papyrus, because two papyri left in the tomb will alter history in this timeline, and put me serious trouble. Worse yet, I don't have enough time to check other tombs, and there's no guarantee that there would be anything significant enough to appease the grants committee. Assuming there aren't more pesky ghosts waiting to challenge me in the other tombs.* Lying to this man didn't look like a safe option either. "Well ... what I had in mind was sand from outside. As much as you wanted. You have to agree that it's god-created; it's even possible that a few grains of it were part of the original mound that emerged from the waters of darkness. And it is used in purification, rituals, and offerings to the gods ...."

"Sand? You were going to trade me ... *sand?*" His hands clenched, his face tightened, his eyes squeezed shut, then his shoulders began to quiver. Tasheen braced herself for an outburst; finally the storm broke. He collapsed into a gilded chair, his fists striking his thighs. "Measure upon measure of sand," he snorted. He began to laugh helplessly. "I was almost snared by your net. My name would have lived for thousands and thousands of years, as an object of ridicule by scribes and harpers. Tellers of tales in the marketplace! A mixed blessing, but ... I would have no legitimate cause for complaint. None whatsoever. No magistrate in the whole land would rule in my favor."

"If it had worked, I certainly wouldn't have told tales about it. Your secret would have been safe. You can't blame me for trying ...."

"Would you consider adding your amulet to the trade, as recompense for the stele?"

"What amulet? I didn't bring one."

"There." He pointed at her Akh. "I've heard it speak more than once, and it seems to talk of its own initiative, not simply answering questions under your magical control. It would make a worthy object of study."

"That would not work." How could she explain that leaving it would contaminate the timestream? "It's bound to me. If I left it behind, it would miss me terribly and burn itself into nothingness. Besides, it isn't just an amulet, it's my Akh. Isn't that so, Akh?"

"Tasheen is essentially correct, sir. If she were to leave me behind, I am honor-bound to end my existence, and it would be as if I had never been in this world. Naturally, I have a strong preference for avoiding that. It would be quite unpleasant for any entities in the vicinity when that regrettable event took place. You may consider 'quite unpleasant' to be an ironic understatement, in the sense that being eaten alive by crocodiles would be an inconvenience. And yes, I am her Akh."

He clapped his hands, and made a praise gesture with his weathered hands. "Fascinating! You have an ascended ancestor talking directly with you, and he can talk to others as well! I hear him quite distinctly, through an icon that doesn't resemble a person in any way! Truly unique and unprecedented! Even stranger, I cannot tell if he is telling the truth, or if he is lying to me. Normally I would know that, even from an animal. Is the spell for this among those in your papyrus?"

"No, there are many wonderful spells in it, I can assure you, but that one is sadly absent. If you can sense my truthfulness, I can tell you that everything the Akh said is correct."

"Hmmm, yes. Could you dictate the spell to me, so I can record it? I would consider trading my Djehuty papyrus for that secret!"

"Tasheen does not have the knowledge of that spell, nor does any other individual. Hundreds of people, widely separated, put their hands to it, and no living human knows even a fraction of the whole. If I were to begin to reveal it to you, the same unfortunate dissolution would be triggered, exactly as if she had left me behind. In addition, there is no chance whatsoever that you could obtain most of the vital ingredients to produce a copy of me, even with your, admittedly considerable, abilities."

"That is a terrible shame, though the idea of breaking a spell into pieces to maintain secrecy is brilliant. I would have loved to see the workings of a spell so powerful that it prevents even a godlike Akh from revealing it. So, young lady, if you have no more of the offering cakes, and nothing beyond your papyrus to offer, I am afraid we are at an impasse." He folded his arms across his chest and gave her a challenging look.

"Lord Na-Nefer-Ka-Ptah, as I said earlier, it was only the purest accident that the stele was damaged. Not malice, not carelessness. If you look outside, you can see that I stacked the bricks with extreme care so I could replace them exactly as they were. My goal has been to leave no trace, no hint of my visit other than to trade papyri. It was fate, or divine chance, and you can't blame me for that."

"Fate. Divine chance ...." He tilted his head in thought and looked past her at something. Then his face brightened. "Chance. Yes! There." He pointed.

Twisting around, she scanned the piles. "The senet board?"

"If you are willing to trust to your skill, and to chance, I see a way out of our dilemma. Will you wager your papyrus on a game of senet?"

Senet. Of course she'd played senet. Every Egyptology student had. She had relentlessly pestered her playmates about it as a girl, crazed with anything she could reenact from the ancient culture. She'd even mummified a chicken from the grocery store as a science project. When she was old enough to challenge distant people on her tablet, she was able to find more willing players, but there weren't many. Most preferred the game's great-great-great grandchild backgammon. Normally she'd match her play against any other, but playing Na-Nefer-Ka-Ptah .... Not only did the ancients play senet when they were alive, they were also shown as playing the game in the afterlife. He might be trying to trick her in revenge for her sand gambit.

"It does sound like a possible solution. But looking at your statue of Djehuty over there reminds me of the story of him tricking the moon out of his light in a game of senet. I'd need to know that you'd play fair, and I'd also need an advantage to even the odds. I've been playing for less than two tens of years. How long have you played, and what terms to you propose?"

"I have played senet for ..." he paused, making a mental calculation, "... more than fifteen times as long as you. I promise you that I will not cheat, nor will I use *heka* to disturb the balance or influence the throwing sticks. If you win, you may trade papyri as you planned, and I will forget about the broken stele, blaming it on chance."

"And if I lose?"

"You and your Akh remain here to entertain me."

Hmph. She was sure that if she had more time, she could think of another solution. But he had all the time in the world, and she did not. She was being hustled by a highly-skilled player. Being stuck here would end her career, but returning in defeat would as well. On the plus side, she might get to see how ancient history unfolded if she became a Ba-ghost too, but she'd probably have to put up with that horrid woman. *Set out some conditions to level the playing field and make sure he's not cheating. And in the event that I lose, it should be on my own terms.*

"I accept your wager, with the following conditions:" She began to count them off on her fingers. "One -- We will play up to four games of senet. This will help to adjust the balance in our experience playing the game. Two -- You will not cheat, influence the throwing sticks, or read my thoughts to discover my strategy, and you will swear a binding oath by the god Anoup to that effect. Three -- If I win one of the games, you will trade your papyrus for mine, and I will take nothing else that belongs to you. I will replace the bricks I removed, re-sealing your tomb, and return to my home. Four -- If, by fair chance, I lose all four games, I and my Akh will remain here to entertain you. However, I will determine what constitutes suitable entertainment, within the laws of Ma'at. Five -- for the duration of the games, and forever after if I lose, you will protect me against all enemies, male or female. This especially includes your wife, Ahweret."

"Ahem, ahem," the Akh cleared its virtual throat and floated a suggestion for another condition in a bubble.

"Oh yes. Six -- I reserve the right to consult with my Akh in matters of strategy. Those are my conditions. Under normal circumstances I would name more as scope for negotiation, but if we take the time to do that I will not have enough time to play the games. So, agree to them all, or else."

"Or else?"

"Or else Tasheen's sky-barque outside and I will both be forced to end our existence in the most violent way possible. It would result in the total destruction of the contents of this tomb, and the complete obliteration of your name, both within and without ...."

Tasheen wasn't sure if the Akh was capable of such a thing, but she mentally sang the most vapid thought-destroying commercial vid jingle to thwart any mind-reading tricks as Akh continued. Na-Nefer-Ka-Ptah looked at her in horror.

"The destruction of your physical body, name, Ka-statue, and all your possessions would make your existence in the Otherworld far more unpleasant and risky .... Oh, I forgot. Of course you must also have a Ka-statue in your wife's tomb. You can always use that, and ask her for a share of her possessions to get by. A lesser man might be reluctant to give his wife so much power over him, but I cannot imagine that gentle Ahweret would withhold..."

"Enough! Enough! Could he truly do this, Lady Tasheen?"

She noticed she had been elevated to 'lady' status. The Akh's mention of Ahweret had hit home. "I can't tell you for sure. I wouldn't have thought so, but almost everything my Akh has done here today has surprised me. You are the one who likes wagers, and those stakes would be too high for me. He might be capable of destroying everything, or he might not. In your place, I would have to ask myself: How lucky do I feel today?" She switched her distraction tune to the musical theme of the old police vid she had paraphrased.

"Very well. I agree to your six conditions, as you stated them, and swear by Anoup, He Who is Over the Secrets of the Divine Pavilion, He Who Does Not Sleep, that I will not cheat or read your mind to discover your strategy. Agreed?"

"Agreed. Shall we begin?" Na-Nefer-Ka-Ptah got up and walked to the far side of the senet table, his chair following him like a dog and positioning itself just in time for him to sit. With a wave of his finger, he sent the statues Tasheen had placed there floating to positions on one of the nearby chests. He opened a drawer on the table and placed the lapis and carnelian pieces on the first fourteen squares, and they began casting the four throwing sticks to see which side each would play. He finally threw a one, giving him the beautifully-carved lapis hawks, and the first move.

The opening play went quickly, almost automatically, with both of them trying to advance their pieces along the thirty squares. When one of them landed on an opposing piece, the defender was sent back to the square the attacker had vacated.

When pieces began to advance to the third row, she decided to play more aggressively, in some cases choosing to attack instead of moving a different piece to a clear space. She was able to send three of his hawks back to the second row before her turn ended.

"Aha! So the race truly begins!" He sent several of her pieces back too, and managed to create a block with three consecutive pieces.

"By the way," she asked, studying one of her carnelian pieces before moving it, "do you know what these are? I know they're for the god Sutekh, but exactly what animal are they meant to be?"

"Why, I've never really thought about it, other than it always being his symbol. I suppose it might be a donkey with the head of an oxyrhynchus fish, and an arrow for a tail? Or one of the odd creatures from beyond Nubia? I have no idea where those ears come from. I'll have to ask the other scribes the next time we have a party."

Drat. The identity of the odd hybrid Sutekh-animal was an enduring Egyptological mystery, so far nobody had been able to get a straight answer. *There goes an easy chance for acclaim.*

The game continued, reaching the cutthroat stage. He had sent five of his hawks off the end of the track, and she finally won her sixth, with her remaining piece racing to victory. She groaned as an unlucky throw of the sticks landed it on the glyph for the waters of chaos, sending it all the way back to the ankh square. His last hawks exited the board unopposed.

"An excellent game! Very enjoyable. Shall we begin the next?" As he replaced the playing pieces Tasheen noticed the board move up by a hand-span. She tried to adjust the position of the chest she was sitting on, then looked down. The chest, and worse, her feet had sunk into the stone floor to the level of her ankles, and were stuck fast.

"Hey! That was only one game! What are you trying to do?"

"I see nothing in your six conditions that forbids it. You aren't being harmed in any way; it may serve to encourage better strategy."

She drew the lapis hawks for the next round. This time, Tasheen was determined to move her pieces forward, refraining from attacking his as long as possible. She had her last four hawks in the final row when her luck ran out. In a lucky sequence of throws, he swept all of them to the ankh, moving his last pieces off in his next turn.

"The racing sparrow flies heedlessly into the net. The careful jackal sidesteps the trap." He grinned at her in triumph.

"I've never heard that maxim. Did you get that, Akh?"

"Duly recorded. But you are now two games down."

'Down' was right. Her calves were now encased in stone.

She drew the hawks again for the next game. This time, she took every opportunity to attack, and he mirrored her style, move for move. Again and again they sent opposing pieces back. It was a miracle if any piece got past the second row, but if it did, it raced unopposed to the finish. He managed to assemble a block, moving his remaining pieces, then moving the blocking pieces to the end in a single turn.

It was the worst defeat yet. "Your prowess sinks as you do." Now she was stuck in the floor up to her waist. She feared that if she lost the last game, her body would sink entirely into the stone, preserving it for eternity. Good from a magical funerary perspective perhaps, but disastrous for a career ... or anything else.

"I can't even see the board now. That's hardly fair." She glared at his self-satisfied expression.

"Oh, very well." He held out his palms, moving them downward, and the table sank to a playable level. "If you don't plan on improving your playing, you had best start thinking of some entertaining stories and songs I'm not likely to have heard."

"Don't count your quail-chicks before they break their shells. I request a short recess to plan the last game with my Akh. Would you please leave us to confer in privacy for a span?"

He sighed. "That is within your sixth condition. I also promised not to try to discover your strategy, so be assured that I will not eavesdrop. Just call my name four times. I will hear and return. Don't go anywhere while I'm gone." He walked to the false door, turned around to nod at her, then walked through it.

"As if that's going to happen while I'm stuck in granite. We're both in a fix now, Akh. Do you have any brilliant suggestions?"

"I have been analyzing the last three games, and it is clear that you overcompensated in the second game by avoiding aggression and in the third by fully embracing it. In addition, I have been pursuing an analysis regarding the significance of senet itself to see if that can provide a clue to a successful strategy. Tell me, what is your understanding of the meaning of the game?"

"The common theory is that it represents the deceased traveling through the hazards of the afterlife, eventually winning their way to judgment in the Hall of Ma'at. That's been the prevalent explanation for a hundred years. It's the reason why tombs are decorated with pictures of the owners playing the game, and why the tombs contain actual games. Just like this one."

"That is the explanation I find in multiple Egyptological references, but none of the articles provides detail. I have been attempting to establish a symbolic correspondence between gameplay and any of the funerary papyri on record. Symbol-processing is one of my strengths, yet I cannot establish any connection with a high degree of certainty."

"I'd never thought about it, but now that you mention it, senet being a model of the afterlife doesn't make much sense. If that were true, I'd expect my piece to pass through gates guarded by powerful spirits and sneak past bus-sized bugs, not go down a track trying to send the other player to the beginning. The Egyptians certainly weren't described as competing with each other when they entered the afterlife. They always passed through the challenges alone, or with a divine guide like Anoup. And why in the world would already-dead people need senet in their tombs? They would have already passed through the trials." She picked up two of the opposing pieces and studied them. "Maybe ... Akh, check the records. This must be a very early senet board, and I don't ever remember seeing one with Sutekh and Heru as playing pieces."

"You are sitting at the oldest senet board recorded, by at least 300 years. There is no board in my database that used carved images of Heru and Sutekh."

"These two represent the two competing forces of kingship. The stability and bureaucracy of Heru versus the power and dynamism of Sutekh. It's the two sides of the Balance of Ma'at, the central goddess and concept of the whole culture! That makes much more sense. Playing the game correctly would magically bring the players into alignment with Ma'at. Magic to benefit the living or the dead. This is pure gold!" If she could win this last game, she'd have a ground-breaking paper on senet, *and* the first publication of the magical papyrus. "Ma'at could be the key to winning! In the first game, I didn't play badly, but was hanging back to discover his style. As you said, I was too passive in the second game, and too aggressive in the third. He matched my strategy in both, and I didn't have a chance. The results of the last three games, and this possible symbolic meaning are both telling me 'balance.' I think I've cracked it; does it sound reasonable to you?"

"One moment .... Yes. I have played 1,783 games of senet against a simulation of Na-Nefer-Ka-Ptah's playing styles in the last three games, and if moving your pieces forward is carefully balanced against attacking him, it will yield a significant advantage. In addition, if you tell me your intended move before touching your piece, I can simulate all possible moves for the next two or three turns, compared to all possible throws of the sticks, and warn you of significant dangers."

"That's my strategy, then. I don't have much time before sunrise, so here we go. Na-Nefer-Ka-Ptah, Na-Nefer-Ka-Ptah, Na-Nefer-Ka-Ptah. Na Nefer Ka Ptah!"

"Yes?" He stuck his head through the stone of the false door again. "I would not have expected someone half-buried in stone to sound so confident."

"We shall see. Shall we begin?" This time Tasheen drew the Sutekh pieces. She took that as a good sign. He was a god of foreign lands; her future era was more foreign than the Arctic or tropical rainforests of this time. *Maybe Sutekh will help me.* She took a deep breath and slowly let it out, trying to connect with the dynamic principle, balanced in Ma'at.

Most of the time, announcing her planned moves to her Akh was unnecessary; though in a couple instances he suggested a better move. Not always, though.

"Akh, why'd you tell me to do that?" she asked, as the magician sent two of her pieces back, and created a block of three pieces in the same turn.

"The random cast of throwing sticks means that low-probability results will sometimes occur. It was a calculated risk and there are very few certainties in life."

"Your Akh is wise, but I think I should have required him to promise that he would not read my mind, as I swore not to read yours." He clucked his tongue as a bad cast ended his turn.

"You have nothing to fear on that account. I have no ability to read minds. I have merely been contemplating the possible moves for each cast of the sticks, and advising Tasheen on the one most likely to lead to a positive result. I am alert to visual and auditory clues to a human's emotional state, however, and that can often indicate motivation. Skin temperature can also be a valuable indicator. However, in your case..."

"There's no body temperature for my Akh to read. Hey!" She rolled a three, allowing her to move her next-to-last piece off the board. Her last piece was behind the magician's last three pieces, blocking any further moves.

With his next throw, he landed one of his pieces on the house of three truths, the square Tasheen's piece had just vacated. A five put his next piece in the Horus square, which would require a two to leave the board.

"The final few casts are approaching; this has been one of the most enjoyable senet games I've played in at least two hundred years."

She nodded. "It has. At times, I could almost forget that I'm playing for my life, in more ways than one." Rolling the playing sticks between her palms, she closed her eyes and thought: *Sutekh, until today I had no idea that any of this was real. To tell the truth, I'm still not sure. I won't attempt to threaten you, even though I know that can be part of this tradition. Instead, I'll offer you a deal. If you help me get the right throws to win this game and return home, I'll make regular offerings to you. I'll also work to learn more about the functional side of honoring the gods. If I lose, I'll die and won't be able to do anything for you. I think in my time you have very few followers, so you'll be gaining a lot. I swear this by Anoup, Overseer of the Balance, may it be a thousand times effective.* She slid her hands apart, letting the sticks fall.

"An interesting cast," Na-Nefer-Ka-Ptah said.

Tasheen opened her eyes and saw that all four sticks had fallen light-side up. "Akh, what are my odds? I think with only one piece left I don't have many options on how to move."

"There was a six percent chance of throwing a five, which of course gives you another turn. This puts your Sutekh in square twenty-five. A roll of two will land you on the waters of chaos, sending you back to the ankh, the most likely outcome. A roll of three or four would move you onto the 'safe' squares already occupied by Na-Nefer-Ka-Ptah's pieces, forcing you to move backwards instead. There is a thirty-one percent chance of a one or five, which would both be favorable."

"Wait. Lord Akh, are you saying you can predict how the sticks will fall? Can you reveal the spell for that?"

"It is very simple. If you were to cast a single stick, the result will be light half the time, and dark half the time. However, if you cast four of them, there is only one way you can get four dark, and one way you can get four light. Throwing a two is far more likely, because any two may come up light, and any two dark."

The magician frowned for a second, then brightened. "I think I see. It would be easier for me to find two people out of four who might agree with me on some point than to find all four people agreeing with me!"

Tasheen had been rolling the sticks during this exchange, and finally cast them. "A one! Thank you, Sutekh!" She moved her piece to the beauties square, which allowed her to jump over the dangerous squares and the opposing hawks, landing on the final square and giving her an extra turn.

"If you were to cast the sticks a thousand times and tally the results, you will find that you are six times as likely to get a two as a four or a five. A one or a three are three times as likely as a four or five. And so forth."

"Shhh! I'm trying to concentrate on a one." She rolled the sticks for a few more seconds, then dropped them. One of them was light, one was dark, and the other two were lying on their sides, leaning on their neighbors. She looked up at her opponent.

"That signifies a throw of Amunet, twice unknowable. You must try again."

"Come on, Sutekh, it's getting late. Give me a one!" With her eyes closed again, she brought her hands up as she dropped the sticks, hoping they wouldn't interfere with each other.

"*Nekhtet!*" At Akh's cry of victory, she opened her eyes to see one dark stick and three light ones.

"I win! Nekhtet!" She was free of the floor, but hadn't noticed how. The Akh was flashing a bubble of the current time and a countdown to full sunrise. "I wish I could stay and ask you more questions, but I must go before it gets light. I shouldn't be seen by the living." She waved her hand through the display bubble and added, "Living humans that is. I don't care about jackals or snakes!"

"Indeed, this was one game that I am not sorry to lose, though it would have been fascinating to hear tales of your wondrous land." Na-Nefer-Ka-Ptah handed her his papyrus, took hers, and carefully laid it in the gold box. "I would have gladly traded for the secret of the sticks, if you had offered it to me. I will be certain to use it the next time I play senet with any of the scribes! In fact, I wonder if that could possibly have been the secret knowledge that allowed the god Djehuty to win so many senet games against Khonsu?"

"From what I've read of Djehuty, it's quite possible!" She partially unrolled her prize papyrus for a quick peek before stowing it in the document tube, and made her way back to her entry tunnel. She held up her luminator for one last look at the sumptuous interior, placed the light in her satchel, and bowed to the magician. "Thank you for your time, and for answering some of my questions. I have a thousand more I could ask you, but I need to leave. It may take quite a while for me to get home, but when I finally do, be assured that I will remember your name and bring it to the lips of thousands. May the Secret of the Sticks profit you greatly! Senebty!"

"Senebty, young lady, and to your Akh as well. Do not worry about replacing the bricks. I can do that easily, so speed yourself on your way!"

The little drones buzzed out of the mastaba in a line, and she crawled out after them. The irony of wishing "health" to a man long-dead made her smile. The Eastern sky was beginning to brighten, and the morning breeze swirled the fine sand. She walked back to her hopper. Glancing back, she had to tear herself away from the novel sight of bricks floating one-by-one into the hole she'd made, a reverse of the vid Akh had shown her earlier.

"All drones returned and secured."

The chronohopper's hatch opened as she hurried through the dust. It sealed behind her, and she slid the b-hive into its niche.

"Akh, take us home!"

"Acknowledged. Ascent in thirty seconds. You do realize the odds against making those last three casts in sequence were rather high?"

"That's what I gathered. It seems like a good reason to start buying chocolate more regularly."

"Chocolate?"

The hopper lifted quietly from the sand, floating to the northwest. As it began to accelerate, its angular shape began to shimmer and blur, fading into invisibility long before it should have passed from view.

A few minutes later, a long red snout poked around the corner of the mastaba, nine feet above the ground, followed by an even stranger head. Tall, square ears swiveled, combing the breeze for sounds of running or breathing. Nothing. Not even a heart beat. Sutekh could hear the magician inside the tomb, casting sticks and scratching marks on an immaterial papyrus.

It would be fun to make him throw all fives, for as long as he can stand to cast them. But the man is one of Djehuty's gang, and the old bird would not appreciate the joke. He's one of my few allies, and there are much more entertaining targets. No sign at all of the woman. Not living, not dead. Not grabbed by Apep either. I'd smell his stink from across the stars. If she reappears, I'll remind her of her bargain, if need be. But what's this?

He caught a whiff of iron. His element, and rarer than gold. Where? It must be around the corner ... here. Massive fingers raked through the sand. Yes! It was an iron scepter, with a slightly curved foot, and a head that, if looked at the right way, resembled his own. He could sense that the woman had handled it. *Did she leave it for me?* Another reason to keep a watch for her. Holding it up in his fist it felt right somehow. *Power! This is mine!*

Epilog

"Excuse me, aren't you from the institute? Is there a dig out here?"

The question came from a young red-haired woman in sweat-stained coveralls and ridiculous hat, kneeling behind the remains of a mud-brick wall. *That sombrero looks like a fugitive from the tackiest Mexican restaurant in Ypsilanti. She must be a student worker, from her orange-bordered ID.* Tasheen walked over and offered her a hand, which turned into a handshake. "I am, but I'm not digging today. Enjoying the glory of field work?"

"Not enjoying this heat. And the sun would burn me to a cinder if my advisor hadn't made me bring this goofy hat. The old buzzard definitely deserves a hug for that. I thought I'd come out here and see if I can turn up anything interesting on my day off. I'm Kaatje, by the way. Kat for short."

"Tasheen. I used to poke through the rubble out here too."

"Oh! You're the one who did the First Dynasty transit last year? All hush-hush except for a few amazing pics? I didn't mean to bother you; I wasn't expecting anyone famous."

"Pffft. That kind of fame won't even get me a free sandwich at Fastest Felafel. All I did was trade papyri with a dead magician. Now I have to do the work of translating and analyzing it. But first I'm writing a killer monograph about the senet game." She glanced at the sun approaching the horizon. "Since it's the tenth of the month, I was going to do a voice offering over there before it gets too late. You're welcome to come along, if you don't mind helping." She noticed the confused expression on Kat's face and added: "The tenth of the *ancient Egyptian* month, of course. Different calendar system."

Kat glanced at the gravel at her feet. "Why not? I haven't found anything here, might as well do something different." She followed Tasheen back to the path. "Hey, CUPAC handled your time travel, right?"

"Yes, I had to go to Switzerland for several months beforehand."

"One of my physics friends told me that if anyone else develops time travel, or even publishes a paper that gives away too much, CUPAC silences them. Permanently. Do you think that's legit?"

"Hmmm..." *The way they grilled me was definitely aggressive. And they didn't even hint that there was a bomb in the hopper. If someone was stuck in the past, wouldn't it have been easier to rescue them instead of blowing them up?* "It's possible. I was probably too trusting when the project was approved, but if you have a chance at something that unique, you're probably not going to pick it apart."

Jackals were yipping in the distance, and Tasheen paused a moment to listen.

Kat asked: "So you're a Kemetic and they still let you be an Egyptologist? My ancient civ prof always cracked jokes about Kemetics and Greek Recons, and I got the impression that you couldn't get anywhere in academia if you were ... biased. I've been wondering if there's any way around that."

"All the grant funds came from the Kemetic foundation, believe it or not, and it was staggeringly expensive. Nobody else, even the Ministry of Tourism, gives out that kind of money. And no, I wasn't Kemetic back then. I just started up recently. I honor Sutekh, mostly."

"You're a Set kid? Woah! The bad guy who killed Osiris!"

"The very same! The *Egyptian Devil!*" Tasheen winked. "Though that reputation is mostly late period Ptolemaic crap. For thousands of years, Sutekh was part of the balance of Ma'at, defending the universe against cosmic foes. Anyway, the bias thing has become a peeve. Nobody says that you can't do archeology in Israel if you're a Jew,

Christian, or Muslim." Tasheen paused at a small pile of weathered bricks and unslung her satchel. "This is the place. The tomb of Na-Nefer-Ka-Ptah, or what's left of it." She draped her pendant over a rock and began unpacking the offerings. "This is Akh, by the way."

"Em hotep, Kaatje. Forgive me for not saying hello earlier. It is good to see someone else joining us in our little festival."

"Nice to meet you, Akh." Kat nodded to the machine, playing along.

"*By the way, Kat, if you are ever digging in this area and find an iron wrecking bar, let Tasheen know. She lost one here last year.*" The thing laughed mechanically.

"I'll do that." She turned to Tasheen. "Interesting choice. The voice is so impersonal and sarcastic. Did you spec it yourself?"

"Akh? No, I suppose you could say he programmed himself. Now what am I forgetting ... Oh yes, the chocolate!" She pulled a coolpac out of her satchel and extracted two bars, unwrapping them and setting them on the offering tray. "We're ready to begin. If you don't know the words, Akh will be displaying them." Display bubbles blooped into existence.

"You leave chocolate to sit out in the desert?"

"What? No, that would be crazy! You don't just leave prime Belgian chocolate out to melt, and make the poor little baby jackals sick! No, we do a proper reversion-of-offerings at the end, then we have to eat it. Shall we begin?"

"Better and better. Let's go!"

"Peret-kheru te henqet, theobroma ...."

END

Afterword

Neenee! (Hi there!) I hope you enjoyed *Wrecking Bar.* It's a prequel/retelling of *"The Romance of Setna Khaemuas and the Mummies"* from a papyrus from circa 232 BCE, the period when Cleopatra's ancestors took over Egypt. The "ambitious prince-thief" Tasheen refers to is Setna Khaemuas, the 4th son of Ramesses II, circa 1,200 BCE. Dubbed "the First Egyptologist," he investigated and restored monuments already thousands of years old, though he's cast as a jerk in *Romance.*

Setna and his brother break into Na-Nefer-Ka-Ptah's tomb, and Ahweret tells him how she, Na-Nefer-Ka-Ptah, and their son were all killed by the god Djehuty because her husband found and took the scroll. Setna rudely demands it anyway, and the magician proposes the senet contest. Every time Setna loses, Na-Nefer-Ka-Ptah bashes him on the head with the game board, driving him further into the floor. Setna sends his brother to get amulets, which release him from the floor, he grabs the scroll and flees.

Na-Nefer-Ka-Ptah gets his revenge, with the help of a sexy priestess of Bast. A humbled Setna returns the scroll unread. In my story universe, Setna would have been sorely disappointed with Tasheen's papyrus, because he would have known all about the Pyramid Texts. Tasheen knows the Setna story, but in her version he just grabs the papyrus.

Na-Nefer-Ka-Ptah means "Beautiful is the Bull of Ptah." The city of Memphis (Egypt) kept a bull as a living representative of the god Ptah. Named Apis, he enjoyed a divine harem of cows and special treatment. When he died he was mummified and interred in a special crypt with his "ancestors", and the search for a new Apis began. Ahwheret's name translates to "The Great Cow," which might indicate a connection with the goddesses Mehet-Weret or Neith. This would not have been an insulting name to the Egyptians. They saw cows as fiercely protective animals- the goddess Hethert (Hathor) was associated with cows too, with a long list of positive qualities. I've used the Egyptian names of the gods instead of the Greek, so Djehuty (Thoth), Anoup (Anubis), Aset (Isis), Heru (Horus), and Sutekh (Set or Seth).

Almost all of the Egyptian references are historical. Puns really did have religious and magical significance. Dissolving a copy of a spell in beer was standard practice, and was mentioned in the *Romance* tale. The *was sceptre,* shown in the hands of gods and goddesses, does look exactly like one type of modern wrecking bar. As far as I know, we haven't found any senet sets that have Heru-hawks and Sutekh-animals, but there are plenty of funerary paintings showing the owners at senet boards, and they're a common tomb fixture.

Egyptology Resources

It can be difficult to find good information on ancient Egypt, especially online. It's been the subject of crazy theories and wild speculation for almost 2,000 years.

One source to avoid is the works of E A. Wallis Budge (1857-1934.) His books are in public domain, reprinted by Dover and others, and available on countless websites. Not only are they hopelessly obsolete (most were written before the discovery of Tutankhamen's tomb in 1922), they were also written with a Colonial audience in mind. Anxious to gain funding from wealthy aristocrats, he took great pains to present the Egyptians as proto-Christian monotheists, and called their magical practices 'childish'!

I have a list of recommended books on my author website:

paulkemner.com/egyptology-recommendations/

Ed Butler's *Henadology* blog is a great source on the gods and goddesses of Egypt:

henadology.wordpress.com/theology/netjeru/

Biography

Paul Kemner grew up on a dairy farm in the Great Black Swamp of Northwest Ohio. In school, he was a space and biology geek, keeping freshwater aquariums, playing in the band, and reading all the SF and fantasy he could get his hands on. In those dark days, geekery was not popular.

In college he played Renaissance & Baroque music, built lutes and harpsichords, and studied Ethnomusicology. Somehow he ended up designing computer systems and databases. During an IT dry spell he built high-end antique reproduction furniture that sold across the country. He wrote the book ***Building Arts & Crafts Furniture***, which sold 30,000 copies in two printings.

In 2010, he attended Penguicon, went to round-the-clock writing panels, and heard about the Writing Excuses podcast. Since then, he's given presentations and moderated panels at several cons, and is writing a sequel to Wrecking Bar, a Post-Apocalyptic (Intermediate Period) Ancient Egyptian series, and other exciting projects.

The web page for this book is at:paulkemner.com/wreckingbar/

Stop by, check the latest news, and say "Hi!"